Groundwood Books / House of Anansi Press
110 Spadina Avenue, Suite 801, Toronto, Ontario M5V 2K4
or c/o Publishers Group West
1700 Fourth Street, Berkeley, CA 94710

We acknowledge for their financial support of our publishing program
the Canada Council for the Arts, the Government of Canada through the
Book Publishing Industry Development Program (BPIDP) and the
Ontario Arts Council.

OA ONTARIO ARTS COUNCIL
CONSEIL DES ARTS DE L'ONTARIO

Library and Archives Canada Cataloguing in Publication
Wallace, Ian
The sleeping porch / Ian Wallace.
ISBN-13: 978-0-88899-826-2
ISBN-10: 0-88899-826-0
I. Title.
PS8595.A566S54 2008   jC813'.54   C2008-901315-8

The illustrations were done in watercolor.
Design by Michael Solomon
Printed and bound in China

THE
SLEEPING
PORCH

Ian Wallace

GROUNDWOOD BOOKS
HOUSE OF ANANSI PRESS
TORONTO   BERKELEY

NE steamy summer night, Brando and his parents deserted their beds for the cots on the sleeping porch at the back of the house. They were hoping to catch the hint of a breeze.

"It's hot enough to wake the dead," his father said.

But in no time at all they were sleeping soundly.

Fireflies flickered.

Cicadas sang.

And shadows shimmied in the grass.

Just about midnight, Brando stirred. He thought he heard a cat yowling in the dark. Then the breeze swirled the dry graveyard earth into dusty funnels and, suddenly, out of the dust came a salty Maine coon cat.

The cat leapt the graveyard wall, soared across the backyard and slipped easily through one of the porch screens.

Brando stared in disbelief.

The cat landed on his cot with a soft thud.

"Hot dog, it's a hot night," the cat yawned. "And I've been asleep forever."

Brando stammered, "H-h-h-how long is...f-f-f-forever?"

"Since the War of 1812 forever," the cat replied and stretched to his full height.

Brando's eyes grew wider. "That's... one hundred and...thirty-four years forever!"

"Y'er darn tootin'," the cat said and flicked his tail. He looked around in the dark. "The night is short. There's no time to waste. Are you with me, matey?"

Brando nodded.

"Then come on board."

Brando stood up on the cot. The Graveyard Cat leapt into the night sky. Brando leapt after him.

The breeze lifted them higher and higher. The air was cooler up there, and Brando and the cat sighed in unison, "Ahhh…"

They glided past other restless families on other sleeping porches, swooped over seagulls perched on clock-tower ledges, and soared over the city that was melting in the heat.

Then they struck out along the coast head on into a cool ocean breeze. Brando and the Graveyard Cat howled in delight.

Up, way up they flew, far beyond the earth, into the darkest void of night.

"Watch this!" Brando called out and did a brilliant back flip through the rings of Saturn.

The Graveyard Cat applauded. "Bravo, matey!" And down, down the cat somersaulted.

"Bravo to you, too, matey," Brando cheered.

The Graveyard Cat bowed low and did a jaunty pirouette.

They flipped and somersaulted and somersaulted and flipped, as they headed due north.

Seals swam beneath them.
And right whales arced over them.
The air grew chillier.
And the ocean swelled, sporting smart white caps.

Soon they saw a shimmering iceberg below them.

The Graveyard Cat called out, "Berg alert!" and dropped out of the sky.

W-h-h-h-o-o-o-s-s-s-s-h-h-h!

They scaled jagged cliffs and slid down whistling slopes.

"Wh-o-o-o-p-p-p-e-e-e!"

"Hot-dig-e-dee!"

The cat broke off two bits of ice and handed one to Brando. It tasted like winter on their tongues.

"Ahhh…," they sighed. "Now that's cool."

While they enjoyed the icy treat, the Graveyard Cat regaled Brando with stories of his life at sea, ending with the tale of how he died.

"Holy cow…you're a hero," was all Brando could whisper at the end.

Many more icebergs floated past. So many more, that before long, they were surrounded by a sea of shimmering ice.

"I'm sleepy," Brando yawned.

"Me, too, matey," the cat yawned.

They curled up and in a nanosecond fell asleep.

The icebergs drifted south, mile after mile.

And as they drifted, they began to melt.

Crevasses appeared where there had been none.

And chunks of ice broke away, splashing into the sea.

When a thunderous crash shattered the night, Brando and the Graveyard Cat awoke with a start. The berg they were riding had split in half.

"AHHH...," cried the cat. "I'm terrified of water!"

"Me, too!" Brando echoed.

"HELP," cried the Graveyard Cat.

"HELP," Brando cried.

But the iceberg kept melting. Brando and the Graveyard Cat watched in horror as it shrank to the size of a snowball.

Brando couldn't keep his toes out of the frigid water.

"H-H-H-E-E-E-L-L-L-P!" they hollered.

Their cries filled the steamy night, echoed along the coast and bounced off clock-tower ledges. They could even be heard on the sleeping porches. Restless sleepers shifted in the summer heat.

"Brando, where are you?" a familiar voice called out.

"At sea, Dad, at sea. Just the Graveyard Cat and me." Brando waved his arms and thrashed his legs.

"Shh…," he heard his father say. "Go back to sleep, son." His warm lips kissed Brando's chilly forehead. "You were having a bad dream."

Brando settled down. The Graveyard Cat, too. And the morning sun edged over the curve of the earth.

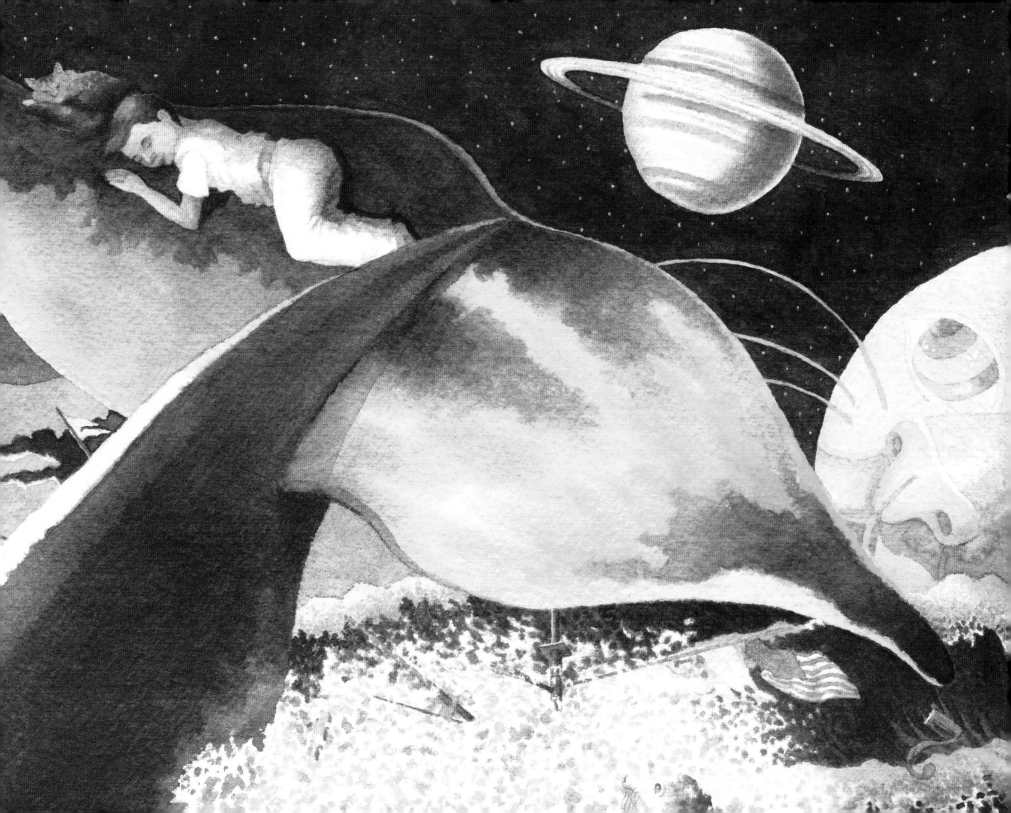

When he awoke, his parents were already up. The sounds and aromas of breakfast being made filled the early morning air.

The Graveyard Cat was sitting on Brando's cot. "Hot dog, that was a hot night," he said.

"And you're one cool cat," replied Brando.

The cat flicked his tail. "See you again, matey. On another night that's hot enough to melt an iceberg."

"Y'er darn tootin'," Brando said.

The cat leapt off the cot, slipped easily through the porch screen, soared across the backyard and passed over the graveyard wall.

A gust of wind came up. Brando waved. And the Graveyard Cat did a jaunty pirouette and disappeared in the dust.

Brando turned to go and stepped in
a puddle of cold water. A shard of
shimmering blue ice glinted from the
floor. He picked it up and looked back at
the graveyard.

"Hey, matey...!" he called out.

But the graveyard was so still, not even
the shadows were shimmying.

He put the shard to his lips.
"Ahhh...," he sighed. "Now that's really
cool." And he went downstairs to begin
another steamy summer day.